Puddle Moon

FOR ROBERT

by Mari Gayatri Stein

with an introduction by Astronaut David Scott

RiverWood Books * Ashland, Oregon

RiverWood Books * PO Box 3400 * Ashland, OR 97520

www.riverwoodbooks.com

Library of Congress Cataloging-in-Publication Data
Stein, Mari, 1947-
Puddle Moon / by Mari Gayatri Stein ; with an introduction by David Scott.
p. cm.
Summary: Megan, her dog Mumbles, Fumbles the cat, and Inches the mouse go outside one rainy night, where
the moon reflected in a puddle invites them to float, fly, and wish, until it is time to go home to sleep.
ISBN 978-0-9793840-0-4 (hardcover)
[1. Moon--Fiction. 2. Rain and rainfall--Fiction. 3. Night--Fiction. 4. Dogs--Fiction. 5. Cats--Fiction.
6. Mice--Fiction.] I. Title. PZ7.S821466Pud 2010
[E]--dc22
2010029247

This book belongs to:

KERPLUNK PLUNK PLUNK

An Introduction from the Man on the Moon

I hope you enjoy this wonderful adventure called *Puddle Moon*, written by my friend Mari Gayatri Stein. The Moon is our friend for many reasons and has inspired countless adventures in science, romance, poetry, and stories just like this one. Sometimes the Moon is a good companion for thinking about our lives and ourselves. It even offers us a light at night.

Once, many years ago, I had a special adventure when I lived on the Moon for three wonderful days during the Apollo 15 expedition. From the Moon, I could see our beautiful blue Earth in the sky, just like you can see the Moon in the sky from here on Earth. Today when I look up at my friend the Moon, it reminds me of good things and happy times.

Join Megan and Mumbles the dog, Fumbles the cat, and Inches the mouse for their magical nighttime adventure. And may you have your own adventures with our bright and shining friend, the Moon.

—David Randolph Scott

KERPLUNK PLUNK PLUNK

Just before sunrise, it started to rain.
As Megan lay in her bed,
she could hear it go
"Kerplunk!" on the roof.

KERPLUNK!

KERPLUNK?

Her dog Mumbles heard it, too,
and opened one eye sleepily.
"Kerplunk?" mumbled Mumbles.

4

The house was quiet,
    except for the soft snores
        of Fumbles the orange cat
        and Inches the mouse.

"Zzzzzzzzz."

Megan snuggled into her pillow and listened to the rain say,
"Kerplunk, plunk, plunk!"
"Kerplunk, plunk, plunk," mumbled Mumbles.
He crawled up the quilt
to rest his cold, wet nose on her shoulder.
Mumbles was looking mischievous.

"Hmmm," thought Megan. "What could be better on a rainy
night than a secret adventure with your very best friend?"
Megan and Mumbles loved secret adventures.

So they slipped out of bed
    past the snoring Inches and Fumbles,
        and tiptoed quietly out the door.

"Shhh," whispered Megan.
        "Shhh," mumbled Mumbles.

The rain was warm.
Mumbles stuck out his tongue
to catch raindrops.

"Yum," mumbled Mumbles.

The moon shimmered in the night sky.

"The moon looks like an ice cream cone," observed Megan.

"Or a yummy bone," mumbled Mumbles.

Awakened by the moonlight's glow, Inches and Fumbles
climbed up on the window sill and peered out.

"The moon looks like a saucer of cream," purred Fumbles.

"Or a slice of cheese," squeaked Inches.

"Let's go out and see," they agreed.

Clouds floated by.
The moon hid.

The rain splashed down. "Plink, ting, ting, plop!"
Megan heard the wind chimes sing. Mumbles heard them, too.

"Plink,
    ting,
    ting,
    plop!"
mumbled
Mumbles.

Puddles were forming everywhere.
Mumbles dashed off to splash around.

Megan followed, jumping and kersploshing like a frog.

The rain slowed to a drizzle.
Suddenly, the night fell silent.
Megan and her friends stared into a puddle.

They watched clouds floating in the puddle's sky.

They saw the moon, tempting as an ice cream cone,

or a yummy bone, or a saucer of cream, or a slice of cheese.

A star joined in.
It glistened beside the Puddle Moon.

A rainbow bird circled in the puddle's sky.

Megan held Mumbles' paw,
and they leaned into the puddle
for a closer look.

It was secret and mysterious down there.

21

Suddenly,
the sky *flashed*
and thunder *crashed*,
sending fat raindrops
plummeting into
the puddle's sky.

With pleasure,
Puddle Moon
shivered and
stretched,
and Puddle Star
twinkled and *twirled*.

"JOIN US!" sang Puddle Moon.

22

Making a grand splash,
Megan and Mumbles and
Inches and Fumbles
tumbled
into the
Puddle Sky
with the Moon
and the clouds
and the
rainbow bird
and the
twinkling star.

"Whee!"
mumbled Mumbles.
"Puddle Moon has
captured the sky.
We can float
and we can fly.

WHEE!"

"Make a wish!" beamed Puddle Moon.
"Make a wish!" mumbled Mumbles.

"LOOK!
Puddle Moon
is *smiling*
at us,"
mumbled
Mumbles.
"Smile back!"

"It's time for sleep," *yawned* Puddle Moon.

"Nighty-night. See you soon."

26

As
Puddle Moon
yawned,
the water
began to
billow
and *swell.*
It *whirled*
and it
swirled,
and it
twirled
our friends
out of
the
Puddle World.

They found themselves sprawled on the lawn and couldn't stop giggling.

"I'm drenched from nose to toes," exclaimed Megan.

"We're soaked from whiskers to tails," her companions chimed in.

Then they giggled and jiggled and wiggled, scattering Puddle Moondrops everywhere.

The rain had stopped,
and the sky was turning gold.
The sun was on her way.

It was time to go home.

Wiping their feet at the door, they tiptoed inside and crept across the carpet, quiet as could be.

"Shhh,"
mumbled
Mumbles.

"Shhh,"
whispered
Megan.

Megan wrapped Mumbles in a big orange towel and rubbed off the mud while he licked her toes.

PTUI!

YUK!

"Yum," mumbled Mumbles.

Warm and cozy, safe and sound, Megan and Mumbles
and Inches and Fumbles cuddled up under the quilt.
They closed their eyes and fell into a dream about puddle skies.
"We love you Puddle Moon," whispered Megan.
"Sweet dreams."

"I love you too," crooned Puddle Moon.

"Nighty-night."